our
generation®

This is Reese's story.

REESE™

THE CURIOUS CASTLE

BY

SUSAN CAPPADONIA LOVE

ILLUSTRATED BY TRISH ROUELLE

An Our Generation® *book*

MAISON JOSEPH BATTAT LTD. *Publisher*

*A very special thanks to the editor,
Joanne Burke Casey.*

To my favorite adventurers,
S, S & O.

Read all the adventures in the
Our Generation® Book Series

CONTENTS

EXTRA! EXTRA! READ ALL ABOUT IT!
Big words, wacky words, powerful words, funny words...
what do they all mean? They are marked with this symbol *.
Look them up in the Glossary at the end of this book.

Chapter One

YOU QUACK ME UP

One Tuesday morning at a little before noon, mail truck #7 rumbled down Figgy Lane. Inside the truck was a large, bright yellow envelope printed with my name and three words handwritten in chunky red letters:

Open right away!

Figgy Lane has plenty of potholes. This makes it a bumpy ride for our mail carrier, Patty Popkin.

The biggest pothole, which is in front of my house, caused the yellow envelope to bounce off the truck's shelf and land right on top of Patty Popkin's mail bag.

"It was as if it wanted to be delivered—and in a big hurry," Patty Popkin told me later that week. "I had a strong feeling that was no ordinary envelope. It held something very interesting."

ॐ ॐ

That very same Tuesday, at about the time that the envelope jumped off the shelf, my three best friends and I were in art class at Rivarosa Elementary School. As we painted, we practiced telling jokes. We were going to do a comedy act for the summer camp talent show.

"Why did the clock get into trouble during class?" I asked.

"Because it *tocked* too much!" Belle hooted.

I continued. "OK, next one. Why was the math book sad?"

"It had too many *problems* in it!" Neve replied.

"Correct!" I praised her. "What did the duck say to the comedian*?"

"You *quack* me up!" Charlotte shouted.

That silly joke made us all start giggling.

"C'mon," I said, hopping up from the table. "Let's wash our paintbrushes so we can be the first ones in the lunch line."

"Reese," Neve said to me, "Pine Breeze Sleep-Away Camp is over a month away! Why are we practicing for the talent show already?"

"That's why we call her 'The Lickety-Split* Kid,'" Belle said, elbowing me lightly.

"Yup," agreed Charlotte with a wink. "She's always in a rush to get things done lickety-split."

"What!?" I said, pretending that I didn't know what they were talking about. "I just want to make sure we have an *amazing* time at summer camp *and* win in the talent show."

"Reese, will you help me learn to sail when we get to camp?" Belle asked.

"You bet," I said.

"It's a tiny boat, but a big pond," Belle said, with a frown on her face. "Since you're the best swimmer on the swim team and you've been sailing before…."

"She's still nervous," Charlotte added, "because the camp counselors* don't actually sit in the boats with us."

"They'll be right on the dock watching everyone sail," Neve said, patting Belle's arm.

"Don't worry," I told Belle, "the counselors will be so close you'll practically be able to smell their sunscreen."

"What if we tip over? Huge fish live in that pond!" Belle said, opening her arms up wide.

Neve, Charlotte and I smiled and shook our heads. Hadn't we just had this conversation the day before? And the day before that? We'd agreed that I would sail with Belle and Charlotte would sail with Neve.

Camp was just about all we talked about. We were beyond excited.

The 4-ever Friends, the nickname we'd given ourselves, were going to be bunkmates. At night we'd snuggle inside our sleeping bags and tell scary stories. During the day we'd make pottery. We'd also play tennis, go swimming and sit together in the dining hall.

We had just about every detail planned for summer camp. That was OK with me. I like to know the scoop* ahead of time and then stick to the schedule.

The only thing left to do was to send in my sign-up sheet and camp fee. In order to make it there by the due date, it needed to be mailed the next day.

"No worries," I said to Belle. "I'll be right there with you in the sailboat."

"Do you promise?" Belle asked.

"No, I *double* promise!" I said.

I didn't realize that it was one double promise I would not be able to keep.

Just a few minutes earlier, Patty Popkin had wedged the big yellow envelope into my mailbox. It was waiting there for me to open it. And when I did, all my plans would change.

Chapter Two

CASTLE FEVER

That night I was sitting up in bed, listening to every word of the story my grandpa was telling me.

"And then," he said in a low whisper, "the princess tiptoed to the secret door. Very slowly she turned the big, heavy, metal key in the lock and CLICK—"

"I knew right where to find you," my mom joked, as she poked her head into my bedroom doorway. "You know how your father says you have 'camp fever' because that's all you and your friends talk about?"

She wagged her finger back and forth from me to my Papa. "Well, I think the two of you have '*castle* fever.' Seriously though, it's time for sleep. It's 8:30 and that's the rule." She tapped the dial of her watch.

"Mom," I said, "can we please have a few more minutes? We're right at the best part of the story!"

My Papa makes up the most amazing stories. They're always about castles and he tells me "one chapter" each night.

Bedtime at my house is like traveling back in time to faraway kingdoms. Castles, hidden tunnels, lords and ladies, fire-breathing

dragons and magical spells are all part of the adventures.

Papa tells me every little bit of the story in such a way that I can imagine the smell of torches burning, hear the knights' metal swords clashing, feel the cool, stone floor of a castle and see the reflection of a full moon shimmering on a moat*.

Because of the stories Papa tells me, I'm crazy about castles and palaces. I've practically "wallpapered" my room with pictures I've drawn of them.

I even wrote a story about castles and entered it in a kids' writing contest sponsored by the Castle Adventures Travel Agency.

The grand prize was a trip thousands of miles away to Europe (pronounced *yoor-ep*) to tour castles and palaces—and *sleep* in one, too! Imagine that!

What would it be like to stand inside a REAL medieval* castle? I often wondered.

"You heard what your mom said." Papa

told me. "It's time to end this story for now. We'll find out what's on the other side of the locked door tomorrow night."

Hmmf! That is what Papa always does. He stops when I just can't wait to hear what happens next.

"Please, please, *please* tell me just five more minutes of the story," I groaned. "I won't be able to get to sleep wondering if the princess finds the stolen crown."

Papa likes to take his time with most things, including storytelling.

"Look at it this way," Papa told me. "Life is like a glass of lemonade. You *could* drink it in one gulp, but you'll enjoy it a whole lot more *one sip at a time*."

"One sip at a time" is not how I do things. It's more like "full steam ahead"! Whatever has to be done, I like to get it done quickly, 1-2-3, so I can move on to the next thing.

Papa says I have one speed: FAST!

"Oh Reese, I almost forgot," my mom

said. "This came for you in the mail."

I was surprised. Mail? For *me*?

It was a large, yellow envelope and looked important. I opened it and found a letter inside.

CASTLE ADVENTURES TRAVEL AGENCY
Where vacation dreams come true!

Dear Reese,

It is my pleasure to inform you that you are the Grand Prize Winner of the Castle Adventures for Kids Creative Writing Contest. Congratulations!

You and one person of your choice will visit castles and palaces in four European countries! You will even have the chance to sleep in one or two. The ticket for your flight to London, England is attached.

Please ask your parent to call us within 10 days so we can make the final travel arrangements for you and your guest. Remember, as part of this prize, you will agree to write weekly travel blogs that will be published on our website, which is viewed by thousands of people around the world each year!

The short story you wrote was funny and smart and full of adventure. It was selected from 1,459 short stories written by kids. Well done! We're looking forward to reading the travel blogs you'll write, too. Our readers will enjoy hearing about travel from a kid's point of view.

Sincerely,
Ms. J. Gilligan
President, Castle Adventures Travel Agency

Chapter Three

FAIRY TALE ADVENTURE

I read the letter three times before I believed what I was seeing.

"I won!" I shrieked with joy. "I never thought in a million billion gazillion years that I would ever actually step foot in a castle."

A glossy* catalog was paper clipped to the letter. The front read, "Castle Adventures in Europe!"

I turned the pages and saw photos of amazing castles and palaces in England, France, Spain and Italy. They were described with words like "enchanting," "enormous," "magnificent*" and "picture-perfect."

I looked up and saw my mother, father and Papa grinning.

"We're going to Europe!" I whooped. "It's a fairy tale traveling adventure for two!"

Suddenly I wished there was a vacuum that could suck those words back in as if I'd never said them. *The trip is for two people*, I thought, *but there are four of us in my family. How can I choose whom to bring?*

I soon discovered that wasn't the only problem.

"Look! Here's your flight ticket for the plane," my mom exclaimed as she pulled a blue piece of paper out of the envelope. "You'll be flying from the Detroit, Michigan airport in the United States to an airport in London, England in the United Kingdom." She handed it to me.

"Wow!" I said as I looked over the ticket. I read the date out loud and gasped. "Doesn't summer camp start the day before that?"

My father checked the ticket, too, thought for a moment and then scrunched up his forehead. "Yes, I'm afraid you're right."

"Oh no-o-o-o-o-o-o," I moaned. "What

will I tell The 4-ever Friends? They're going to be so mad at me."

"Disappointed maybe," Papa said, "but not mad."

My mother added, "They'll understand."

"I suppose," I said glumly*. But I didn't think they would.

✿ ✿

It was impossible for me to sleep when Papa turned off the lights that night.

Who will help Belle learn to sail? I wondered. In my mind I saw her sitting dejectedly* on the dock at camp, with no partner for boating.

And then I pictured Charlotte, Belle and Neve at arts and crafts, painting with watercolors, making friendship bracelets for each other, and performing in the camp musical.

That was followed by thinking about all three of my friends playing water balloon tag, zinging water balloons at the other campers and each other. And since I have a pretty good imagination, I could see them dripping wet, laughing hysterically and having a blast.

Stop thinking! I scolded myself. *I'll never get to sleep if I let my mind keep racing ahead to things that haven't even happened.*

I forced myself to not think about summer camp. Instead I began fretting* about how to choose who would go on the big trip with me.

If I asked my father to go on the trip, Papa and my mom would miss out. If I chose

23

my mother, my father and Papa would be left out.

No matter what I decided, two people I love wouldn't be able to go.

And will my friends think I'm ditching them for something better? I thought. *I want everyone to be happy (including me!). How in the world can I do that?*

❧ ☙

The next afternoon, when I came home from school, I noticed that my sign-up sheet for camp was still on the kitchen counter. My mom hadn't mailed it.

At the same time, I felt a flutter of excitement in my heart—I was going to Europe!

The strange thing was, my homework assignment that day was to draw a map of Europe. It was a project for my favorite class, which is Geography.

Geography didn't interest me that much until Papa moved in with us last year after

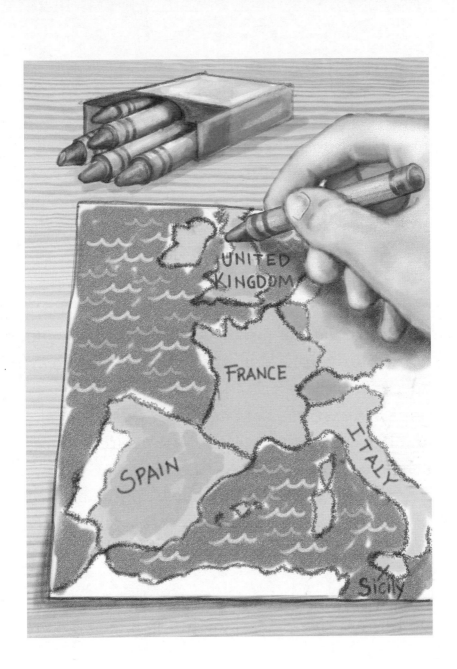

Nana, my grandmother, died.

Papa is always reading about different countries. He uses the facts he learns to make up his bedtime stories.

Papa's adventurous spirit has rubbed off on me. He says I'm like a sponge, soaking up the stories about people and places around the world.

When Papa was young, he had the time of his life exploring lots of countries. He once told me that he'd promised Nana they would go to Europe one day to experience their own adventures together.

I knew that if Nana were still alive, she and Papa would travel to all the exciting places he creates stories about.

Sicily would be at the top of his list because his mother was born there. *He'll never go now,* I thought sadly. *He wouldn't want to go alone.*

Papa could be my "one guest," but it still seemed unfair to my mom and dad.

My summer vacation was getting so confusing. *If only I could bring my whole family,* I thought.

Aha! Maybe my family could buy two more tickets and we could *all* go. Then no one would be left out.

"Yes!" I said. "That's it!" I ran down the stairs to find my mom and dad.

My dad listened to my plan and then put his hand gently on my shoulder. "Thank you, Reese, for thinking of a way to keep the whole family together for this big trip."

"But," my mom added, "summer is our busiest season at the bicycle shop. Since we own it and do all the bicycle repairs ourselves, there's just no way for us to get away."

"So you wouldn't mind if I asked Papa? You won't feel left out?" I asked.

"You two will have such a great time," my dad said.

"We'd better warn Europe," my mom teased. "Here comes The Lickety-Split Kid and

Papa, too!"

That night at bedtime, Papa finished telling me the last chapter of his story. As usual, I begged him to keep going and start a new story.

"Just a few more minutes!" I cried. "Let's just start the next story."

"Nope, it's 8:30. The rule is the rule," he said, as he fluffed up my big, yellow pillow and pulled the zigzag comforter up to my shoulders.

I asked him about going on the trip.

He nodded his head slowly. "That is really nice of you to invite me."

A trip with Papa would be so much fun. My mood soared.

Then it dropped when he said, "But I don't know if that's such a great idea."

Papa passing up a chance to travel? I looked at him with surprise.

"It's a big responsibility," he said. "What

if something happened to you, like if you got sick?"

I knew what might convince Papa: "You speak French and I'm learning to speak Spanish. Perfect, right?"

"Let's think it through," Papa said. "Have patience, Reese."

Patience smay-shence, I thought. I must have made a frownie face.

"I'm just not sure," Papa said. "Let me give it some thought."

I knew what *that* meant. "Let me give it some thought" is usually parents' code for "if we wait long enough maybe she'll just forget about it."

In other words, "no."

Chapter Four

DECISIONS, DECISIONS

Crabby. That's how I would describe my mood the next morning as I pushed cinnamon and apple oatmeal around in my bowl without eating any.

"Did you wake up on the wrong side of the bed?" my mother asked.

I didn't understand what she meant. I can only get out of bed on one side because the other side of the bed is against the wall.

My mom noticed the puzzled look on my face. She laughed. "Waking up on the wrong side of the bed means that you woke up feeling grouchy."

"In that case, I guess I did," I admitted. "Not only can our whole family not go on the castle adventure trip, I can't even find *one person* who will go with me. Plus, now the sign-up for camp has passed, so I'll miss out on that, too."

"It will all work out," my mom told me. "Just wait and see."

Waiting and seeing is very hard for me. But I agreed to try.

❧ ❧

At lunchtime, Charlotte, Neve, Belle and I were walking down the hall to the school cafeteria.

"Everybody sent in their sign-up sheets and camp fees, right?" Charlotte asked.

"I sent mine in last week," Neve said.

"Me, too," said Belle.

Everybody stopped walking. I looked up from my sweater, which I'd been picking at for no good reason. My three friends were staring at me.

"Reese?" Belle asked.

"Um...oh..." I began. "I wanted to tell

you something exciting that happened. But it's not as exciting as camp, of course. I mean it is, but in a different way..."

"What is it?" Neve asked.

I finally was able to tell them about the writing contest, the letter and the grand prize. And then, to try and make the situation sound not so great, I added, "But now I might not be going on the castle adventure at all."

Silence. They looked confused, then angry.

"So you're not going to camp!?" Charlotte asked, her face turning red and blotchy.

"What happened to The 4-ever Friends sharing a cabin, telling scary stories at night and learning tennis?" Neve asked.

And then Belle asked the question that made me saddest of all: "Who is going to be my sailing partner?"

"I'm ready, Papa!" I hollered, as I jumped into my bed that night.

We were starting a new story. That meant new characters and new mysteries to be solved.

"Once upon a time," he began, "there was a…"

He told me about a special girl who wanted to know everything she could about other countries.

"Just like me!" I told him.

"Yes, exactly like you," he said. "She

dreamed about castles and adventures and travel," he continued.

"Me, too!" I said. I liked the story already and it had only just begun.

"And her grandfather was the same way," he said. "A once-in-a-lifetime chance came up for them to go on a trip together."

"Hold on! Is this a story about us?" I interrupted.

"You're always in a hurry to get to the end," Papa continued, with a twinkle in his eye. "So, as I was saying...they pack their suitcases and off they go to explore the world!"

"Papa!" I cried, giving him the biggest hug ever. "We're going? Together?"

"I always promised your grandmother we'd travel someday," he said. "But we never got to do that. Here's a way to keep my promise by taking her granddaughter, the talented writer!"

"Hooray!" I cheered, and then added in a teasing voice, "There's just one problem."

"What's that?" he asked, frowning.

"Unlike the girl in the story," I replied, "I don't have a suitcase to pack."

"Problem solved!" my dad said. He entered my room pulling a long handle attached to something big on small wheels. It was wrapped in colorful paper. My mom followed behind.

"For you, Reese!" she said. "We are all so proud of you."

A small orange tag with a cute cat face on it dangled from the handle. A piece of paper was taped to the wrapping paper. Handwriting on it read:

For your world tour!
xoxox,
Mom, Dad and Papa

Chapter Five

ROLLING ALONG

I ripped off the wrapping paper and discovered it was a sparkly suitcase in my favorite color: bright blue. The wheels on the bottom let it spin around and roll back and forth.

Putting my hand behind my head and my nose in the air, I pretended I was a model. I rolled the suitcase down the hall as if I were leaving for the trip right then. Boy was it ever heavy! That could only mean one thing. My mom and dad had packed a few things for me.

ZZZZZZip! Inside the suitcase was everything I needed for travel: a lime green camera, travel journal, map of Europe, pink-and-white airplane-patterned handbag, matching eye mask and passport case. There was also a pink travel case filled with a toothbrush, toothbrush holder, floss and travel-sized shampoo, conditioner and hand cream.

My parents thought of everything. They even packed crackers, gum and gummy snacks, plus a polka-dotted neck pillow for sleeping on the plane.

"One more thing," my mom said, bringing a gift bag from behind her back.

I pulled the orange tissue paper out of the top. Inside was a smallish blanket that was the color of vanilla ice cream and about as long as I am tall.

"It's a cozy blanket to keep you warm on your travels," my mom said.

"Thanks, Mom," I said, rubbing the fuzzy blanket on my cheek. "It's so soft."

My friends weren't mad at me for long. Actually, they weren't mad, just disappointed, like my Papa had said they might be.

The four of us patched* things up the next day. Neve told me that she understood. Charlotte said she'd go, too, if she had the chance. And Belle said she couldn't wait to hear all about the castles I visited.

They all said they'd miss me sooooooooooo much. That made me feel good because I'd miss them a lot, too.

❧ ❧

A month flew by and as quick as a blink, it was the last day of school. The day after that, my friends were leaving for camp.

Charlotte's mom was driving all the girls and had asked if I wanted to come along. I jumped at the chance. The van was packed with all their duffel bags, sleeping bags and trunks. There was hardly room for us kids.

Once we got to Pine Breeze Sleep-Away Camp, Charlotte, Neve and Belle checked in and we made our way to the cabin. It was in a forest overlooking a pond.

It was even better than what we'd been imagining all winter. Inside the cabin were three bunk beds. Two were already all set up.

One bed was for the camp counselor. The other bed—the one that would have been mine—had a piece of paper taped above it with lots of hearts and swirls and flowers doodled around the name "Francesca."

Whoever this Francesca person was had

moved right in and made herself at home. There was a sleeping bag covered in pink flowers, a puffy blue pillow and even a teddy bear.

"That's a good idea," Neve said. "Let's all make name tags for our beds."

"Yeah, let's!" Belle agreed.

I helped my friends set up their beds and store their trunks underneath. And then we took pictures of us all in silly poses.

Soon we met their bunkmate.

A girl with shoulder-length, light brown hair bounced into the cabin. Right away, she introduced herself as "Francesca." She was friendly and funny and spoke with an accent that was beautiful to hear.

Francesca told us that she was a long way from home. She was going to camp while her parents were teaching a summer class at a college nearby.

"Where do you live?" I asked.

"Oh, the Pink Castle," she told me, as if it was no big deal.

I glanced* at my friends, who all seemed surprised.

What kind of nonsense is this? I thought sourly. *Is she trying to impress everybody?*

I guessed that she had heard about my castle trip and thought she could outdo me by saying she lived in one. Hmmfff!

"A *pink* castle...how *curious*," I said, meaning that it was quite unusual.

Before I could ask more about it, Charlotte's mom announced that it was time for us to leave. Everyone gave me hugs. Even Francesca threw her arms around me.

"Goodbye, Reese!" my three friends called out from the cabin doorway. I watched them wave their arms wildly back and forth until Charlotte's mom and I were down the curvy path and out of sight.

I plunked myself onto the backseat of the minivan, missing my friends already. I looked beside me at a green gift bag on the floor.

"Oh no!" I gasped. "I forgot to give

this present to Charlotte, Belle and Neve!" I'd brought them a mini* globe so that when I sent postcards, they could find the country each postcard was mailed from.

Charlotte's mom said it was A-OK for me to run back and drop it off. As I was skipping along the path, I heard loud giggling coming from the cabin. Then huge shrieks of laughter.

What's so funny? I wondered, as I climbed the stairs to the cabin door.

There were my friends, all sitting on Francesca's bed and gathered around her. Francesca had her hands in the air like she was in the middle of telling a story. Belle was wiping tears of laughter from her cheeks. Neve was holding her stomach.

The four of them were laughing so hard, they never even saw me slip the bag inside the door.

I couldn't help fretting about the future of The 4-ever Friends. *Will they end up liking the new girl more than they like me?*

Chapter Six

OFF WE GO

The next night, Papa and I were buckling our seat belts on the plane when the pilot's voice came over the speaker.

"Hello folks! Our flight time to London is a little under eight hours. We'll be cleared* for takeoff in just a few moments, so please make yourselves comfortable."

Our castle adventure was about to begin!

We were on an overnight flight, but I was so excited, I was sure I'd never be able to sleep. Just in case, I put the polka-dotted pillow around my neck and got cozy under my travel blanket.

"I hope I didn't forget to pack anything," I said to Papa.

Papa laughed. "Reese, you had your blue

suitcase packed three weeks ago! And you checked it at least five times after that."

"I guess you're right," I agreed.

I stretched my neck to see out the window, which was two seats over. The seats were empty.

"Excuse me," I heard someone beside Papa say.

I looked up to see a girl about my age standing in the aisle. Her hair looked like she had been in a windstorm and her cheeks were rosy. She blew a puff of air out of the side of her mouth to get a strand of hair off of her face.

She was holding her tickets in one hand and a bag in the other. "I think those are our seats," she said, jerking her head and pointing with her nose to the two empty seats beside me.

"Oh, sure," I said, as Papa and I stood and moved into the aisle to let her and the woman she was with into the row.

She plopped herself into her seat. "Whew! I didn't think we were going to make it! Our taxi got a flat tire on the way here and the driver had to fix it. That's why we're late. I'm Jessica, and this is my mom."

"Hi! I'm Reese and this is my grandpa," I said. "I'm glad that you didn't miss the plane."

As it turned out, they could have fixed *four* flat tires and they still would have made it to the plane on time.

We heard the pilot's voice again. "Sorry folks, there's been a delay and we'll get moving just as soon as we can."

We didn't leave the runway* for more than an hour. Even though I was anxious to get to England, the time passed quickly. I learned that Jessica was returning to London, which is where she lives.

We were gabbing so much that I switched seats with Jessica's mother so we could talk better.

Jessica rattled* off a list of places that Papa and I should visit. I got out my pen and journal and jotted down her suggestions.

"Wait, wait, slow down," I said. "What was that last thing you told us to make sure we do in London?"

"Ride on the famous red double-decker buses," she said. "They make stops all around the city at most of the places I told you about," Jessica said.

I filled four pages with sightseeing tips from Jessica. "We'll need roller skates!" I joked. "Because we only have four days to see all these places."

Papa piped up, "I used to be a pretty good roller skater back in the day."

Jessica and I both giggled, thinking about Papa roller-skating around England.

I must have dozed* off. The next thing I knew people were gathering their suitcases and bags from the overhead bins.

The pilot's voice came back on the loudspeaker. "On behalf of the captains and crew, thank you for flying with us today."

"Papa!" I said, tapping his arm. "We're here! We're at the London airport!"

"What? Who? Huh?" he said, as his eyelids fluttered open. "Already?"

"Yep," I said, getting up. "We'd better hurry. I bet the Castle Adventures Travel Agency shuttle bus is waiting outside right this minute. They're taking us to our hotel. Then they'll drop us off at our first castle tour."

We followed Jessica and her mother to

the baggage carousel. The large machine was already dumping suitcases down a conveyor belt* and onto a shelf that was moving in a huge circle. I spotted our suitcases and rushed over to grab them.

After we said goodbye to Jessica and her mother, we sat on a bench outside to wait for the shuttle bus. Ten minutes ticked by on my watch but there was no shuttle bus in sight.

Hurry up! I thought.

"Let's take a look at the letter from the travel agency again," Papa said.

I dug it out of my travel bag. "It says that it was supposed to be here at...this can't be right! An hour ago!"

"Looks like we missed the bus," Papa said calmly.

"That means we're also going to miss touring the castle!" I cried. "What are we going to do now?"

Chapter Seven

RIGHT UNDER OUR NOSES

I heard a familiar voice behind me. "You're coming with us, that's what you're going to do."

I whirled around. "Jessica! I thought you left already."

"We did," Jessica's mom said. "Then Jessica remembered that the plane took off late and you might have missed your ride. So we turned around. Now you have your own personal shuttle bus to the hotel."

Thank goodness for new friends, I thought.

Once we checked into the hotel and dropped our suitcases off, Papa and I took Jessica's advice and traveled around London on the top level of a red double-decker bus. The first stop? A castle tour at the Tower of

London, which was fascinating.

Then it was on to Buckingham Palace. The tour bus guide explained that is where The Queen performs her official duties. There are many royal thrones there, including the ones used by The Queen and Prince Philip.

The Ballroom is so enormous it could fit 84 double-decker buses inside. Do you know how The Queen walks into one of the rooms? Through a hidden door from her private apartment!

I noticed that some things in London are not at all the same as where I live. For example, cars drive on the left side of the road, not the right. The museums are free. You can walk right in and look around. There are tall red telephone booths all over the city. Paper money and coins are different, too.

We were on a mission to find eight things: a sticker that says "London" for my suitcase and seven noses for Papa.

That's right! The "Seven Noses of Soho"

are models of human noses that are stuck onto buildings. With so many things on my must-see list, I didn't know why Papa would want to find a bunch of noses.

We looked for the first nose for over an hour, trekking up and down and around streets, checking our map and wondering if we were walking in a huge circle. And we were right. It was sticking out of a brick wall and it had literally been *right under our noses* where we had begun looking!

By the end of our visit, we had only found two of the seven noses. As usual, Papa had been correct. Hunting for the noses let us see areas in London we might have missed.

We must have walked five miles every day that we were in London, including a walking tour to Windsor Castle. When we returned to the hotel each night, I got the laptop computer out and wrote about all the things we did and saw. Before I knew it, my first travel blog for the newspaper had come together.

* * * * * * * * * * * * * *

Around the World with Reese
First stop: England!

Hello, readers! I am excited to write my first travel blog to you from London, England. After my Papa and I arrived by plane at Heathrow Airport, our trip began by riding on the top level of a red double-decker bus!

When we toured Windsor Castle, the world's oldest and largest occupied castle, we decided that "1,000" is a magic number. Windsor Castle is one of the residences of Her Majesty The Queen and has been the home of British royalty for almost 1,000 years. The shields and armor of over 1,000 knights are on display. Can you imagine how many rooms are in this castle? If you guessed about 1,000 rooms, you are right!

During our very regal* day, we also "took" afternoon tea (as they say here in England). A restaurant offered us each our pick of 12 teas.

I chose English Breakfast tea and Papa chose Earl Grey tea. The teas arrived in pretty white china teapots and the servers showed us how to pour the tea through small strainers that rested on the teacups. The strainers keep the loose tea inside the pot from getting into the cups. Next came a metal stand that held plates on three levels. The plates were arranged with tiny decorated cupcakes and pastries, and dainty* finger sandwiches with the crusts cut off.

The next day was filled with art. First we went to the National Portrait* Gallery and I took part in a workshop where I made a clay model of a queen I saw in a painting there. Then we went to a cartoon museum, where Papa and I learned how to draw cartoon characters of ourselves. Funny and fun!

On our boat cruise down the River Thames, we noticed carved stone lion heads on the walls above the water. The tour guide told us that they're about 150 years old and they're said to warn people about floods. The saying is "If the lions drink, London will sink." In other words, watch out if the water level gets too high.

A plane, a bus and a boat, all in just a few days. Tomorrow we'll board a train for—where I'm going next is for you to guess! Here's a hint. Wish me *bon voyage* (safe journey)!

✳ ✳ ✳ ✳ ✳ ✳ ✳ ✳ ✳ ✳ ✳ ✳ ✳ ✳

I'd added five photos I'd taken in London to the e-mail I sent to the travel agency. *I hope Ms. Gilligan and the travel agency like it,* I thought.

৵ ৶

There had been lots of things I didn't have room to include in the blog, like how Papa likes exploring places that are off the beaten track* and somewhat unusual.

I'd wanted to stick to the schedule we'd planned. It made me worry that all the time spent exploring less famous places meant that we wouldn't get to the sights I wanted to see.

Did I mention that Papa loves people? He's so chatty, he makes friends with everyone. Charlotte, Belle and Neve like him so much that they think of him as part of their families, too. They gave him the nickname "Mr. Papa."

For example, one morning we were leaving for the next country on our tour (you didn't think I was going to give it away yet, did you?). Papa's laid-back, take-it-easy attitude made me impatient. He was having a long, long chat with a man who was sweeping the sidewalk in front of his sandwich shop.

As they kept talking and talking, it got later and later. I tugged on Papa's sleeve and pointed to the train ticket, as if to say, "We'd better go or we'll miss the train we're taking in less than an hour."

But Papa, with his enjoy-life-one-sip-at-a-time attitude, smiled and continued listening to the story the man was telling him. Finally, Papa shook the man's hand and said goodbye, but there was no time to spare*.

We huffed and puffed as we ran the five blocks to the train station, pulling our suitcases.

Just as we dashed into the station, I saw the closed doors of the train blink open and shut and open again.

"Hurry, hurry!" I yelled, mostly at myself because Papa was already in front of me.

When we got so close we could almost touch the train, the doors slammed firmly shut. The train jolted* forward and my heart sank.

Chapter Eight

UNDERWATER TRAVEL

Five seconds later the train stopped a few feet from where it started. The doors opened and a man in a uniform waved his hand as if to say "Come in! Quickly!"

We were barely in our seats when the high-speed train began whooshing down the tracks. Close call!

I pulled a sewing kit out of my handbag. I'd decided to find a patch in every city I visited and then sew it on my travel blanket.

The first fabric patch I was going to decorate my blanket with was embroidered* with London's famous, huge clock tower. Many people call it Big Ben, but that's actually the name for the bell that's inside the tower.

The train ride also also gave me time to

catch up on writing in my travel journal and jotting notes on postcards to my parents and friends at camp.

"Seeing you writing jogged* my memory," Papa said, opening his laptop. "I checked my e-mails while you were in the shower earlier. Look!"

I read the words on the computer screen out loud:

To: Reese
From: Ms. Gilligan
Subject: Fantastic work!
   Dear Reese:
      The first blog you wrote is just what our agency hoped for—interesting and fun. Our readers will enjoy hearing about Windsor Castle and all the extra sights you saw along the way.
      Your writing shows that you're having an incredible adventure! Keep up the great work and keep the terrific photos coming, too.
   Ms. Gilligan
   Castle Adventures Travel Agency

I felt on top of the world all the way to—Paris, France.

The next four days were Wonderful with a capital W. We did and saw so many interesting things.

When I sat down to write the next blog, I remembered how Papa described the colors, sights, smells and tastes in his bedtime stories so I could imagine the scenes. I decided to include some of those details in my blogs, too.

"OK," I said. "Here it goes." I hit the "send" button and the e-mail was instantly on its way to Ms. Gilligan.

✳ ✳ ✳ ✳ ✳ ✳ ✳ ✳ ✳ ✳ ✳ ✳ ✳ ✳
Around the World with Reese
Next stop: France!

Bonjour, readers! Hello! Imagine traveling in a train through an underwater tunnel from

England to Paris, France! That's where Papa and I are now, and that's how we got here.

The first thing on our must-see list in the City of Light was the Eiffel Tower. We did a little "trick photography" there. My Papa asked me to stand in front of the tower and bend my elbow with the palm of my hand facing the sky. In the picture it looks like I'm holding the Eiffel Tower in my hand! Then we walked up 704 steps to the top of the upside-down cone-shaped iron monument*. It's over 1,000 feet high (there's that magic number again!). From there we saw the most incredible views of the city.

Later on, we toured Paris and visited the Arc de Triomphe, which is a grand* arch that is over 160 feet tall and 150 feet wide. When we were so tired we couldn't walk another step, we stopped for dinner at an outdoor café. We watched people drift by and it was the perfect ending to another perfect day.

The next night, we slept in a real castle that was built in the Middle Ages*. It is said to have once been given away as a wedding gift and later sold for 2,000 gold crowns. The castle is *vraiment magnifique* (magnificent)!

Papa and I took a pastry class, which taught us the secrets of making delicious croissants and éclairs. A croissant is a curved roll that's flaky, sweet and often eaten for breakfast. An éclair is a soft, log-shaped pastry that is filled with delicious melt-in-your-mouth cream and iced with chocolate frosting. Just thinking about how yummy they tasted makes me hungry.

Au revoir! (That's goodbye in French.) I will be sorry to leave France the day after tomorrow, but excited to continue on to—oh, you didn't think I was going to spoil the surprise, did you? Where I'm going next is for you to guess!

✳ ✳ ✳ ✳ ✳ ✳ ✳ ✳ ✳ ✳ ✳ ✳ ✳

Before we left that beautiful French city, there was one last thing that Papa and I wanted to do. We headed to the Louvre Museum to see three great ladies. They aren't real women—

they're works of art.

There's the *Mona Lisa* (one of the most famous* paintings in the world), the *Venus de Milo* (a mysterious goddess) and the *Winged Victory of Samothrace* (a statue of a woman with wings).

On our way there, we stopped in a small shop, where I spotted a sticker with an Eiffel Tower on it for my suitcase.

"*Bonjour!*" Papa said to the employee at the cash register.

"*Comment allez-vous?* (how are you?)," the store clerk asked in French. Then he said in English, "I'm Pierre. I work here after school. Where are you from?"

Oh no, here we go again! I thought. *Papa makes friends everywhere we go. We're about to get into another long conversation!*

I hoped the museum would not close before this dilly-dallying* was over.

Papa explained where we live while Pierre put the sticker, a fabric patch embroidered with the word "France" and a French flag, and four postcards in a white paper bag.

"I've never met anyone from there!" he said excitedly. "Can you show me?" He pulled a map of the world out from under the counter and unfolded it. There were hundreds of purple dots on it.

Pierre used a purple marker to put a tiny dot on the spot I pointed to on the map. "I like to keep track of the places that travelers who visit this shop come from."

"You've met a lot of people!" I told him.

"Oh yes," Pierre replied. "I hope to travel to many of these places one day. But for now, I enjoy meeting nice people like you so I can put a friendly face with each place."

Pierre is a very interesting person. I would have liked to talk to him more, but there were a few customers behind us in line. *I wonder what dots they will help Pierre put on his map,* I thought.

We did get to the Louvre Museum to see

the three famous ladies. I noticed that only one of them is smiling. (Figure out which lady is smiling by asking a parent to help you look up the works of art on the museum's website. Or take a guess and check the answer on page 105.)

(Figure out which lady is smiling by asking a parent to help you look up the works of art on the museum's website. Or take a guess and check the answer on page 105.)

That night, as Papa and I were heading back to the hotel, I saw a group of four girls my age walking on the sidewalk along with a couple of parents. Three of the girls were laughing like crazy at a joke one of the girls was telling.

It reminded me of Francesca, of the curious Pink Castle, and my three friends at camp.

I wondered, *Have they been having a blast waterskiing and playing ping-pong and volleyball? Will I be left out of all their jokes when I go back to school in the fall?*

Has Francesca taken my place in The 4-ever Friends?

Chapter Nine

TRAVELING COMPANIONS

A day later, Papa and I took a train to our next destination*—Barcelona, Spain!

Planes are sometimes a faster way to get to where you are going, but trains let us see the countryside. We whizzed past Spain's steep mountains and brilliant fields covered with bright, golden sunflowers.

Still, I was excited to start exploring by foot. The instant the train stopped in Barcelona, I leapt out of my seat. "Let's go," I said.

"One sip at a time," he said with a wink.

"OK," I agreed. "Sorry. I just can't wait to see Spain!"

We hopped off the train and headed for the street.

Suddenly, I had a funny feeling that

something wasn't right.

"Oh no! I left my travel blanket on the train!" I cried as I spun around to see if the train had left. It was charging down the tracks.

"I'll call the train company and see if they can find it," Papa told me.

<small>Click-clack</small> click-clack click-clack click-clack click-clack. I heard the quick sound of a woman's high-heeled shoes on the tiled floor, coming closer.

There was a light touch on my arm. I turned and saw a hand with pretty red fingernails holding my blanket.

When I gazed* upward, I recognized the smiling woman who was handing the blanket to me. She had been sitting on the train in the row behind us. Now she was out of breath from running to catch up with us.

"¡Oh *gracias!* ¡*Gracias!*" I thanked the woman in Spanish. I hugged the soft blanket close to my chest.

"*De nada* (it's nothing/you're welcome),"

she said as she turned and waved goodbye.

And that was how our adventure began, with more kindness, this time in Spain!

It was also my first conversation in Spanish there. All the studying I had done was paying off. I was able to read some of the menus at restaurants and order in Spanish and to listen to people talking and understand some of what they were saying.

I had a couple of funny "oops!" moments, too.

For example, one day I awoke at sunrise, excited to get going and see the sights. I peeked out the window and saw that I wasn't the only one up so early—the streets were filled with activity.

On our way to breakfast, I spoke to the hotel manager in Spanish and told him that I was surprised to see how many people were already in the city.

He looked rather puzzled, but smiled politely.

Later on that day, when I realized I'd actually said that I was surprised to see how many *penguins* were already in the *bathtub*, I giggled out loud.

❧ ❧

I was sure that I hadn't heard Papa correctly when he suggested taking a catnap. "Naptime?!" I said to Papa. "There are too many things I want to do and see in Spain."

"Not naptime, Reese, it's siesta time,"

Papa explained. He prounced it SEE-eh-steh. "In some parts of Spain, the afternoon is a relaxing part of the day to take a break, or enjoy a walk or a cup of coffee with friends.

I looked at my list of places that I still wanted to explore in Barcelona. "How about this?" I suggested. "You can get a coffee, we'll take a nice walk and skip the nap thing?"

Papa gave me the thumbs-up.

"OK then, let's go," I said. "We have places to go and people to meet."

"You mean," he teased me, "*you* have places you want to go and *I* have people I want to meet."

"Exactly! And a blog to write," I reminded him. "So let's skedaddle* and start exploring!"

✳ ✳ ✳ ✳ ✳ ✳ ✳ ✳ ✳ ✳ ✳ ✳ ✳

Around the World with Reese
Next stop: Spain!

¡Hola! readers. Hello! My first day in

71

Barcelona, Spain, was pretty "sweet." Papa and I went to a chocolate museum. We learned all about chocolate, made chocolate lollipops and decorated them with spices, fruits and nuts. And the best part of all? The chocolate tasting, of course!

The next day we took a train to the countryside. There we survived staying in a castle that was built by a king over 1,000 years ago (there's our magic number again). I say survived because this castle-turned-hotel is said to be "haunted." The ghost is supposedly dressed in clothes from long, long ago and only hangs around outside the door of one certain room. Luckily it wasn't our room! I don't know if it's a true story, but it's sure a good story.

The castle is amazing. It's built on top of a hill that's 1,500 feet above the walled village. That was just one of over 1,000 castles and palaces in Spain (1,000 again!). If only I had a few more years here to explore them all ☺.

Believe me when I tell you flamenco

dancing is good exercise! Papa and I took a lesson while we were in Spain. It was very hard to get the footwork of the dance right, but we had fun trying, stamping our feet and clapping our hands. The flamenco dancers' costumes were colorful, ruffled dresses that flared out and swished around as the dancers twirled to the music of the flamenco guitarists and musicians.

Don't be alarmed if you go to a Spanish restaurant and your waiter brings you a very tiny plate of food. It's *tapas* (pronounced TAH-pahs), which means snacks in Spanish. And because they are small, you can sample many kinds of tapas without getting too full. They can be hot or cold, but they're always scrumptious!

¡Adiós! That's goodbye in Spanish. Any idea where I'm off to? Where I'm going next is for you to guess! I'll give you a clue. The country is shaped like a boot.

✳ ✳ ✳ ✳ ✳ ✳ ✳ ✳ ✳ ✳ ✳ ✳ ✳

Some of the most famous artists in the world are Spanish. We saw works of art by Salvador Dalí and Pablo Picasso at the National Art Museum of Catalonia.

But you don't have to be famous to attract a crowd. We saw lots of people gathered around two artists who were drawing with sidewalk chalk on a large cement space near Park Güell.

The artists were drawing colorful flags from every country. As people walked by and admired the huge square made up of many flags, they tossed coins on their country's flag. That is how the artists earned money.

Art is everywhere you turn in Spain, including statues, sculptures, drawings and paintings.

One day, we saw a man in Las Ramblas, an outdoor market, standing in front of a canvas on an easel. He was dabbing* bursts of colors onto the canvas with his paintbrush.

Before our very eyes, the canvas was soon filled with a scene of bouquets at the flower shop, crates of fruits and veggies at the market and a woman pushing a baby carriage.

It was amazing to watch everything we saw in real life be created in paint.

Chapter Ten

IT'S A SMALL WORLD

To: Reese
From: Ms. Gilligan
Subject: Our readers thank you!

Dear Reese:

Fan mail for you is piling up here. People are writing to say how much they enjoy hearing about your travels through the blog, and how much they are learning, too.

Reading about the places you're describing makes them want to travel. That's what we like to hear—your blog is good for our business!

You are a good photographer—more pictures please!

Ms. Gilligan
Castle Adventures Travel Agency

What terrific news! I hoped that my parents and friends were reading the blog and had received all of the postcards I'd sent to them.

Camp was over, so I mailed the postcards I'd just written to Charlotte, Belle and Neve to their homes. I imagined Patty Popkin putting them in my friends' mailboxes. I also wrote my last blog.

✳ ✳ ✳ ✳ ✳ ✳ ✳ ✳ ✳ ✳ ✳ ✳ ✳ ✳
Around the World with Reese
Next stop: Italy!

Buongiorno, readers! Hello! If you guessed that the country that's shaped like a tall boot is Italy, you are correct.

Today Papa and I visited Castel dell'Ovo, which is on an Italian island that overlooks the city of Naples. If you think of the country's boot shape, the island is just above the front of the ankle.

The castle has a funny nickname, which is the "Castle of the Egg." My new friend, Lucia, whom I met at a café by the castle, explained the nickname. According to legend, there was once a famous poet who said he'd placed a magical egg under the bottom of the castle. When the egg broke, disaster* would come to the city of Naples.

We also traveled to an olive grove, which is like an apple orchard except with rows and rows of olive trees. We went there to see my mother's olive tree. That's right! For my mother's birthday, my dad had given her a certificate that said she was the proud parent of an adopted olive tree.

The owners of the grove sent my mom two cans full of oil that was made by pressing the olives that grew on the tree. We dipped fresh bread in it and it was *delizioso* (delicious).

At the grove, Papa took a picture of me hugging my mom's tree. There was a tag on the tree with my mom's name plus the tree's birth date —which was over 150 years ago!

Venice, Italy is like no other place I've ever been. There are two ways to get around: by foot or by boat. There are no cars there because the roads are narrow canals, which are waterways between buildings.

A gondolier waved to us from a gondola, which is a flat-bottomed boat with two ends that point up. The gondolier stands at the back of the boat and steers the way through the water with a long oar. He asked Papa and me if we would like a ride to our hotel. As we glided through the canals, we saw many grand *palazzi* (palaces).

I was surprised when the gondolier "parked" the boat and pointed to where Papa and I were staying—an 800-year-old palace!

This is my last stop on the castle tour and my last blog. May your adventures be filled with as much fun as mine. *Buon viaggio* (have a good journey)!

✳ ✳ ✳ ✳ ✳ ✳ ✳ ✳ ✳ ✳ ✳ ✳

While we were in Venice we also took a ferry to explore two islands nearby. First we went to Murano, where artists have blown glass treasures for hundreds of years. One of the prettiest patterns is created with teeny-tiny glass flower shapes. This design is called

79

millefiori which means "thousand flowers." (Yes, another 1,000!)

From there we took a ferry to Burano, which is known for its beautiful lace and for houses that are painted in every color of the rainbow.

I also became something of a gelato expert while I was in Venice. What that means is that I ate a lot of tasty Italian-style ice cream.

The next day, in his usual friendly way, Papa struck up a conversation with a man and woman eating at the table next to us in a restaurant.

"*Grazie*," Papa thanked the woman for passing the pepper to him.

Pretty soon they were all laughing and acting like they'd been friends for years.

It was nice to see Papa enjoying himself, but I was also beginning to get impatient. We'd planned to go to a play at a famous theater. It was hugely popular. I knew that if we didn't get there soon, the tickets might be sold out.

The chef came over to our table. He was a happy man, named "Mario," who was wearing a white jacket. He pulled up a chair and sat down with us.

I sighed. The chef was definitely going to stay awhile. Even after the man and woman paid their check and left, the chef kept right on talking with Papa.

I knew this was Papa's vacation, too, but

I felt antsy*. *One sip at a time*, I reminded myself. *Enjoy things as they come.*

Suddenly the chef stood up, pushed back his chair and went back to the kitchen.

Hurray! We might still make it to the play! I cheered silently.

Just as quickly he returned, holding up two bright white cooking aprons. He announced, "Let's go, you two! Enough talking!"

Geez, and I thought I was impatient. What's this all about? I asked myself.

I shot a quick look at Papa.

Papa shrugged. "All I said was that I've never made a pizza."

"In!" Mario pointed with his thumb to the kitchen. "It's time for your private lesson on how to make Italian pizza," the chef said with a wink.

It turned out that not only is Mario a talented chef, he's a great teacher, too. He taught Papa and me how to throw pizza dough into the air and spin it around until it stretched

82

out into a flat, round circle. Next we put the crust on a pan and added sauce, cheese and toppings.

Mario let Papa use a large paddle to slide the pizzas into the wide oven. The aroma of our pizzas baking was a wonderful smell I will never, ever forget.

When the pizzas were done, Mario, Papa and I sat down at a table and began to devour hot, delicious slices of pizza. A few customers came in and Mario invited them to try Papa's first-ever pizza. More people joined us and

soon it was like a big party.

I felt glad that I hadn't rushed Papa out of the restaurant to get to the play. We would have missed one of the highlights* of our trip.

As we walked back to "our palace" that night, Papa and I stopped at a little market where I found a perfect sticker for my suitcase. It was round, with a picture of a pizza on it, and it read:

If you love Italy,
you have good taste.

Something *very* unexpected happened on the last weekend of our vacation. It started out by Papa and I deciding to flip a coin. We were trying to choose where we would go for the last three days of our trip before we flew back home.

We were playing it by ear*. For a person like me who likes to have everything all planned out ahead of time, this was a step in the right direction!

I wanted to go to Rome, Italy. Papa

wanted to go to Sicily, to the small town where his mother was born.

I checked my purse to find a coin to flip. Empty. Papa fished around in his pockets and pulled out a tissue, a brown wallet, his phone, the hotel key and a crumpled receipt from last night's dinner.

Excuse me," Papa said to a man and woman who were standing nearby. "It seems we need a coin to flip. Would you happen to have one we can borrow?"

"Salvatore," the woman said to her husband, "do you have a coin to lend these nice people? I just used my last one."

Salvatore patted his coat pockets and then dipped his hand in and pulled out a shiny coin that had the number 2 on one side. He handed it to Papa.

"Thank you," Papa said to Salvatore. "We'll give it right back."

Papa and I agreed that if it landed with the 2 facing up, we'd go to Rome. If the 2 was facing down, we'd go to Sicily.

Papa rested the coin on his finger and flicked it high into the air with his thumb. It spun 'round and 'round as it fell down and landed on the sidewalk. No number 2.

I don't usually like losing, but this time I was OK with it. I knew this trip would mean a lot to Papa.

Papa started chatting with the couple. He must have realized it was going to be a long conversation, because he gave me some money to run into the market and get snacks before we left for Sicily.

"If you see our daughter in there," joked Maria, who is Salvatore's wife, "please tell her we're growing old out here waiting for her."

"I will," I promised, as I pulled open the glass door of the market. I grabbed two oranges and stood in the long checkout line.

That's when I was surprised to notice a girl who looked *exactly* like Francesca right ahead of me in line!

Couldn't be her, I thought. *No way.*

I swayed to the right to get a better look at her face. *Don't be silly*, I thought. *The chances of meeting Francesca in another country at a market are about one in a million!*

Maybe the girl sensed me staring at her, because she suddenly twirled around.

"Reese?!" cried the girl who looked like Francesca, and actually *was* Francesca. "What are you doing here?"

Chapter Eleven

THE MEMORY BLANKET

This time it wasn't Papa having a long conversation with a new friend. It was me. I explained that we were going to visit the place where Papa's mother was born.

Francesca told me that she and her family had been visiting friends in this city, but were headed back to the Pink Castle the next day.

I still wasn't sure what that meant. It didn't sound like Francesca was bragging.

"We loved the postcards you sent to camp, and we looked up all the places on the mini globe," she told me. "Charlotte, Belle and Neve missed you so much. They talked about you all the time."

"Really?" I asked. That made me feel so good.

"There you are," Papa said, as he entered the store with Salvatore and Maria.

"We thought you got lost," Salvatore said.

"Reese," Papa said. "I just happened to mention to Salvatore and Maria that we were headed to Sicily. And guess what? They live just a few miles away from your great-grandmother's house!"

"That's right," Salvatore said. "We'd just love to have you over for dinner while you're there."

"Mom and Dad," Francesca said, "you won't believe this, but this is Reese, the girl I told you about who won the castle adventures trip."

Salvatore and Maria looked very surprised. "I'm so happy to meet the person Francesca has told me such nice things about," Maria said.

"It's a small world," Papa said, smiling from ear to ear.

"It sure is," Maria agreed. "Many people

in your family still live in our town. I bet they'd just love to come and meet you."

"Yes, yes, we insist," Salvatore said. "We'll have a traditional Sicilian feast* at the Pink Castle."

"Let's see," Maria said, tapping her chin as she thought. "We'll invite your mother's family…cousins, babies, and family friends."

I was amazed. *Is this really real?* I thought. *I'm going to a pink castle? I'm going to meet Papa's family—our family? And all because Papa asked to borrow a coin?*

Thank goodness for friendly, relaxed, take-life-one-sip-at-a-time Papa.

෴ ෴

We took a train and a ferry to get to Sicily. It was a lot of traveling, but worth it.

For starters, when we arrived at the Pink Castle, I laughed right out loud. There was no moat as I had imagined. It didn't have a drawbridge* or grand entrance.

90

It wasn't fancy or majestic*. The Pink Castle was just a small house that was one story high. It might have been described as plain if it wasn't for the color—a beautiful shade of light pink! It certainly was a curious castle!

A sign in the front of the house, hanging from a post, was swinging in the wind. Peeling paint, which made it look like it was a hundred years old, read:

Benvenuti al Castello Rosa

Papa told me the meaning of the words: Welcome to the Pink Castle!

Francesca, Maria and Salvatore welcomed us and excitedly swept us into the backyard. It was set up with long, rectangular tables covered with green-and-white checked tablecloths. Pretty wildflower bouquets in glass vases decorated each table. I'd never seen so much food in my life!

Lots of people of all ages were already there and everyone wanted to hug Papa and me. I bet I got about 200 hugs.

Everyone was laughing and talking and sharing stories about my great-grandmother.

A cousin of Papa's told us about her family now and how the town had changed. It was all so interesting.

Papa told them about his life, the job he had as a firefighter for over 27 years and about his children. He pulled a picture of my grandmother out of his wallet and pointed to it. "That was my beautiful bride," he told his family.

"Reese looks so much like her," Papa's cousin said.

"She has her grandmother's brains, too," Papa said with a twinkle in his eye, "and she got the love of storytelling from me. Did you know she's a famous writer?"

When the conversation finally turned to another topic besides me (thankfully!), my eyes

drifted around to the buzz of activity, the yard, house, family and friends.

The Pink Castle is small and certainly nothing like the magnificent castles we've been touring, I thought. Kings and queens had not lived there. There were no secret tunnels or knights in armor. But somehow, this castle seemed just as enchanting.

❧ ☙

On the plane ride home, after devouring* the mac-and-cheese lunch served to us by the flight attendant, I snuggled under my travel blanket.

In my mind, I pictured all the souvenirs* I'd brought home. A hand-blown glass heart necklace from Murano, Italy for my mom, a keychain with an itty-bitty double-decker bus dangling from it for my dad and hand-painted fans from Spain for Charlotte, Belle and Neve.

A thought popped into my head. I'd brought home souvenirs for everyone but me!

Not exactly, I thought, glancing at the colorful patches I'd sewn on my travel blanket. I realized that the times I'd shared with Papa were the best souvenirs of all. I was literally wrapped in wonderful memories.

I had patches from famous tourist attractions that had been on my "must-see" list. The unusual sights and out-of-the-way places stuck out in my mind, too.

The round patch from Spain reminded me of the jugglers and acrobats who entertained* people in a crowded park.

A patch with a French flag made me smile. Papa and I had rented bikes one afternoon and stopped for a picnic lunch on the coast of France.

The square patch from London made me think of seeing the lights of the clock tower at night, the red double-decker buses and a little building in Trafalgar Square that I might have walked right by. Papa had pointed it out and told me that people say it was once the smallest police station in the world. It's so tiny, just one person could fit inside!

Thank goodness for Papa, who likes to "take the road less traveled."

Chapter Twelve

THE HOMECOMING PARTY

When I got home from the airport, the first thing I noticed was a big paper poster on the front door. It read:

Hurray! You're home!
We missed you, Reese!
(And you, too, Mr. Papa!)

I recognized right away that the poster was decorated with Belle's handwriting, Neve's puffy hearts and Charlotte's flowers with swirly centers. My friends were all waiting inside.

My mom had made a chocolate cake (my favorite) with fudge frosting (Papa's favorite). My dad had squeezed fresh lemons and made a pitcher of pink lemonade.

I was so thrilled that they'd thrown a homecoming party for us, I thought I'd burst.

Everybody was talking at once and wanting to know every detail about our trip. I told them about the castles, how a woman rescued my blanket, how I learned to make croissants and about the big celebration in the town where Papa's mother came from.

"It sounds like a dream come true," Charlotte said.

"It was," I told them. "Except for when I was practicing my Spanish and told the hotel manager that I was surprised to see how many penguins were already in the bathtub." My friends thought that was hilarious*.

I learned that the whole time my friends were at camp, they (including my new friend, Francesca) checked the camp post office every day to see if there was a postcard from me.

"You'll be very proud," Neve said. "Belle got her sailing certificate!"

"It took me a whole week to get up the

courage to get on the boat," she admitted.

"All that matters is that you did it. I'm so proud of you, Belle!" I said, wrapping my arms around her and pressing my cheek next to hers.

"Reese," Papa asked me, "did you tell everyone our idea? I just ran it by your mom and dad and they think it sounds like fun."

"You are all invited," I explained to my friends. "On the first Friday of every month, Papa and I are hosting International Night. Each party will celebrate one country."

"Your parents and brothers and sisters are invited, too," Papa added.

"We'll host a Parisian Pastry Class where you'll learn to make éclairs and a Spanish Fiesta with flamenco dancing lessons," I said.

"And a British afternoon tea with finger sandwiches," Papa added.

"And don't forget the Sicilian feast with lots and lots of hugs," I said.

"What a fun way to learn about people in other countries," Charlotte said, and everyone agreed.

I'd planned to use all the notes in my travel journal to help plan the parties.

Before my friends left, Neve told me, "Reese, don't go winning any more contests before camp next summer."

"That's right!" Charlotte added. "Francesca is coming again and the counselor said we could fit another bed in our cabin."

"We'll be The 5-ever Friends!" Belle said.

I pointed my finger in the air. "I know just what we can do for the talent show! We can start practicing—"

I stopped in the middle of my sentence when I spotted Papa at the kitchen counter. He was refilling his glass with pink lemonade.

Oops! There I go again, rushing to what's ahead! Seeing Papa had reminded me that camp is a whole year away. In the meantime...I think I'll enjoy life as it comes, one sip at a time!

Glossary

Many words have more than one meaning. Here are the definitions of words marked with this symbol * (an asterisk) as they are used in sentences.

ages, as in the "Middle Ages": *the period of history in Europe from about the year 500 to about 1450*

antsy: *impatient, restless*

belt, as in "conveyor belt": *a long strip of rubber or metal (as on a baggage carousel) that moves objects from one place to another*

cleared: *given permission*

comedian: *a person who puts on a show by telling jokes*

counselors: *people who watch over children at a camp*

dabbing: *adding in light, quick strokes*

dainty: *small and pretty*

dejectedly: *sadly*

destination: *a place someone travels to*

devouring: *eating hungrily*

dilly-dallying: *wasting time for no good reason*

disaster: *a terrible event*

dozed: *slept lightly*

drawbridge: *a bridge across a ditch or moat* that can be raised up so people can't cross it*

ear, as in "playing it by ear": *doing something without planning it*

embroidered: *decorated with thread to create a design*

entertained: *put on a fun show*

famous: *being known by many people*

feast: *a large meal, usually to celebrate an event*

fretting: *worrying*

gazed: *looked thoughtfully*

glanced: *looked quickly*

glossy: *smooth and shiny*

glumly: *sadly*

grand: *large and very fancy*

highlights: *the best parts, events that stand out in a person's mind*

hilarious: *very funny*

jogged, as in "jogged Papa's memory":
   caused a person to remember something

jolted: *moved suddenly*

lickety-split: *quick*

magnificent: *grand**

majestic: *magnificent**

medieval: *like or from the Middle Ages**

mini: *small*

moat: *a ditch filled with water that*
   surrounds a castle

monument: *a famous building*

patched, as in "patched things up":
   repaired damage, made feelings better

portrait: *a drawing, painting or photograph*
   that shows only a person's face or
   their head and shoulders

rattled: *talked quickly*

regal: *royal style suitable for kings and queens*

runway: *the straight, flat ground that*
   airplanes take off from

scoop: *the latest information*

skedaddle: *hurry*

souvenirs: *items kept as reminders of*
    places that were visited

spare, as in "no time to spare":
    nearly not enough time

track, as in "off the beaten track":
    unusual places, or places where most
    people might not go

Answer to the riddle in Chapter 8:
Who is the "famous lady" in the
Louvre Museum who is smiling?
It's Mona Lisa!

Light up the night with a
Castle Fever Fireworks Show!

Reese's mom says that Reese has "castle fever."
Reese has practically wallpapered her bedroom
with all the drawings of castles she's created.
Help her finish this picture
by adding brilliant color.

Simply make a copy of the drawing
on the next page, gather a few crayons
or markers, and you're ready to light up the sky
with a celebration fit for royalty. Fill in each
space with colors that match the letters:

P = purple
O = orange
R = red
G = green
Y = yellow
B = black

Or, mix it up and choose your own colors.
If P = pink, your castle will be the same shade
as Francesca's castle!

Power of a Girl Initiative

For every Our Generation doll, outfit or accessory you buy, a portion of sales goes to Free The Children's Power of a Girl Initiative to help provide girls in developing countries an education—the most powerful tool in the world for escaping poverty.

Did you know that out of the millions of children who aren't in school, 70% of them are girls? In developing communities around the world, many girls can't go to school. Usually it's because there's no school available or because their responsibilities to family (farming, earning an income, walking hours each day for water) prevent it.

Free The Children has now built more than 650 schools which educate more than 55,000 children throughout the developing world. Free The Children also builds and fosters sustainable villages through healthcare, water programs and alternate income projects for moms and dads that give girls the opportunity to get the education they need.

The most incredible part is that most of Free The Children's funding comes from kids just like you, holding lemonade stands, bake sales, penny drives, walkathons and more.

Just by buying an Our Generation doll or accessory you have helped change the world, and you are powerful (beyond belief!) to help even more.

If you want to find out more, visit:
www.ogdolls.com/free-the-children

 FREE THE CHILDREN
children helping children through education

Free The Children provided the factual information pertaining to their organization.
Free The Children is a 501c3 organization.

this is **our** story

We are an extraordinary generation of girls. And have we got a story to tell.

Our Generation is unlike any that has come before. We're helping our families learn to recycle, holding bake sales to support charities, and holding penny drives to build homes for orphaned children in Haiti. We're helping our little sisters learn to read and even making sure the new kid at school has a place to sit in the cafeteria.

All that and we still find time to play hopscotch and hockey. To climb trees, do cartwheels all the way down the block and laugh with our friends until milk comes out of our noses. You know, to be kids.

Will we have a big impact on the world? We already have. What's ahead for us? What's ahead for the world? We have no idea. We're too busy grabbing and holding on to the joy that is today.

Yep. This is our time. This is our story.

www.ogdolls.com

this is **my** travel story:

_____

_____

_____

_____

_____

_____

_____

_____

_____

_____

_____

_____

About the Author

Susan Cappadonia Love lives in Milton, Massachusetts with her husband, Scott, and daughters, Sophie and Olivia. Together they went on their own mini castle adventure in London, England and Venice, Italy—and even slept in a palace just like Reese did!

This story also came to life because of all the wonderful people who contributed their creativity and vision, including Joe Battat, Dany Battat, Karen Erlichman, Sandy Jacinto, Loredana Ramacieri, Véronique Casavant, Véronique Chartrand, Jenny Gambino, Natalie Cohen, Lisa Armstrong, Joanne Burke Casey and Pam Shrimpton. Thank you to Sarah Marotta, Paulina Brito Flores and Carrie Haigh for their help with translations.

*In addition to **The Curious Castle**, Susan has also written ten other books in the Our Generation® Series, **A Song from My Heart**, **The Circus and the Secret Code**, **Magic Under the Stars**, **The Most Fantabulous Pajama Party Ever**, **The Jukebox Babysitters**, **The Dress in the Window**, **The Sweet Shoppe Mystery**, **The Mystery of the Vanishing Coin**, **Stars in Your Eyes** and **One Smart Cookie**, as well as other children's books.*